Meet A.R.F.

Adapted by **Michael Olson**
Based on the episode written by **Bob Smiley** for the series created by **Harland Williams**
Illustrated by **Premise Entertainment** and the **Disney Storybook Art Team**

ABDOBOOKS.COM

Reinforced library bound edition published in 2020 by Spotlight, a division of ABDO, PO Box 398166, Minneapolis, Minnesota 55439. Spotlight produces high-quality reinforced library bound editions for schools and libraries. Published by agreement with Disney Press, an imprint of Disney Book Group.

Printed in the United States of America, North Mankato, Minnesota.
092019   012020

DISNEP PRESS
New York • Los Angeles

THIS BOOK CONTAINS
RECYCLED MATERIALS

Library of Congress Control Number: 2019942739

Publisher's Cataloging-in-Publication Data

Names: Olson, Michael; Smiley, Bob, authors. | Premise Entertainment; Disney Storybook Art Team, illustrators.
Title: Puppy dog pals: meet A.R.F. / by Michael Olson, and Bob Smiley; illustrated by Premise Entertainment, and Disney Storybook Art Team.
Other title: meet A.R.F.
Description: Minneapolis, Minnesota : Spotlight, 2020. | Series: World of reading level pre-1
Summary: Bob introduces the pugs to A.R.F., a robotic dog programmed to clean up any messes the puppies make; but A.R.F. isn't programmed to clean up after himself.
Identifiers: ISBN 9781532143946 (lib. bdg.)
Subjects: LCSH: Puppy dog pals (Television program)--Juvenile fiction. | Puppies--Juvenile fiction. | Robotic animals--Juvenile fiction. | Inventions--Juvenile fiction. | Readers (Primary)--Juvenile fiction. | Pug--Juvenile fiction.
Classification: DDC [E]--dc23

Spotlight
A Division of ABDO
abdobooks.com

Bingo and Rolly play. Bingo jumps on the chair. Rolly flies into the air!

Bob comes home.
He has a surprise.

It looks like a dog.

But it is not soft and furry.
It does not have a wet nose.

"I call him A.R.F.," Bob says.

"A.R.F. stands for

AUTO-DOGGIE
ROBOTIC FRIEND."

A.R.F. was made to clean messes.
Now Bob will have more time to play.

Bob goes to work.

Bingo says, "We love to make messes."

A.R.F. says, "I love to clean messes!"

Bingo and Rolly get to work!

Books fall.

Papers fly.

Stuffing spills.

It will take Bob a long time to clean.

But not today!
"A.R.F. loves to clean!" says A.R.F.

A.R.F. wants to clean more messes.

But the puppies are tired.
What will A.R.F. do now?

A.R.F. spots another mess to clean!

A.R.F. chases Hissy. Hissy runs away!

Food spills.

Plants fly.

Books fall.

Now the house is messier than before!

But A.R.F. was made to clean the pups' messes. He does not clean his own.

The pups will have to clean this mess.
"Let's do it PUPPY DOG–STYLE!"
Bingo says.

Bingo and Rolly clean the mess.

Bingo starts the washing machine.
Rolly pours in the soap.

The puppies run out to play.
The washing machine overflows!

Rolly plays a game.

Bingo goes for a run.

The alarm goes off.
Bob will be home soon!

Bingo and Rolly run inside.
Suds are everywhere!

They run to the washing machine.
More suds pour out!

They run up the stairs.
But the suds keep coming!
What will they do now?

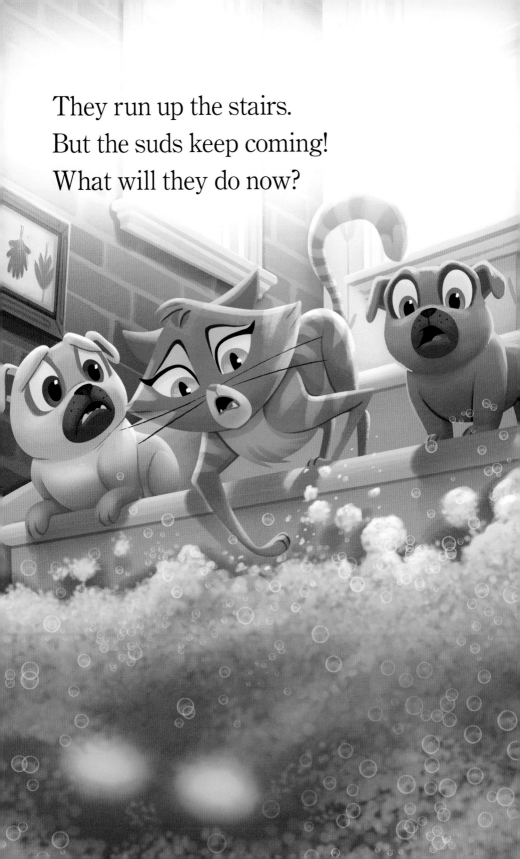

A.R.F. will clean the puppies' mess!
"Bow to the wow!" says Rolly.

Bob gets home.
There are no messes to clean.
Time to play!